DAVID SUZUKI

THERE'S A BARNYARD IN MY BEDROOM

ART BY

Eugenie Fernandes

David Suzuki Foundation

GREYSTONE BOOKS

DOUGLAS & McINTYRE PUBLISHING GROUP

Vancouver/Toronto/Berkeley

Greystone Books
A division of Douglas & McIntyre Ltd.
2323 Quebec Street, Suite 201
Vancouver, British Columbia
Canada V5T 4S7
www.greystonebooks.com

David Suzuki Foundation
2211 West 4th Avenue, Suite 219
Vancouver, BC V6K 4S2

Library and Archives Canada Cataloguing in Publication
Suzuki, David, 1936–
There's a barnyard in my bedroom / David Suzuki; Eugenie Fernandes, illustrator.
Co-published by the David Suzuki Foundation.
ISBN 978-1-55365-329-5
I. Natural history—Juvenile literature. I. Fernandes, Eugenie, 1943–
II. David Suzuki Foundation III. Title.
QH48.S894 2008   J508   C2007-905575-3

Editing by Kathy Vanderlinden
Jacket and text design by Jessica Sullivan
Jacket illustration by Eugenie Fernandes
Printed and bound in China by C & C Offset Printing Co., Ltd.
This book is printed on Ancient Forest Friendly paper, using 100% recycled content.
Distributed in the U.S. by Publishers Group West

We gratefully acknowledge the financial support of the
Canada Council for the Arts, the British Columbia Arts Council,
the Province of British Columbia through the Book Publishing Tax Credit,
and the Government of Canada through the Book Publishing Industry
Development Program (BPIDP) for our publishing activities.

A RAINY DAY HIKE

WAKE UP, JAMIE," says Megan. "It's Saturday. Today we go on our nature hike with Daddy."

"Mmff," Jamie says into his pillow.

Suddenly, Megan hears a pit-a-pat on the window.

"Oh no! It's raining! What'll we do, Dad?"

"No problem," says Dad. "We can take our hike in the house."

Jamie's eyes fly open. "How can we do that?"

"We can start right here, with the sheets and blanket on your bed. Where did they come from?"

"Oh, I know!" says Megan. "The sheets are made of cotton, and the blanket is made of wool. Cotton comes from a plant, and wool is sheep fur. Right, Dad?"

"Right. Now, guess what's inside your pillow."

"Feathers!" Jamie cries. "They fly out when Megan and I have a pillow fight. What bird do they come from, Dad?"

"Probably ducks or geese—or even chickens. Okay, hikers— to the kitchen."

(3)

"What else comes from chickens?"

"Eggs!" says Megan. "And cheese and milk come from—"

"Cows!" cries Jamie. "We have a whole farmyard in our refrigerator!"

"Carrots and peas and bananas come from plants," Megan says.

"Does all our food come from animals and plants?" Jamie asks.

"Yes, all the food we need comes from nature," Dad says. "And do you know what? We also have a forest in the house. Can you find it?"

(5)

"I know, I know!" says Jamie. "The floor and chairs are made of wood from trees."

"Yes, your dresser is made from pine trees. And the dining-room table is made from oak trees."

"That's where acorns come from, too," says Megan.

"So maybe there were squirrels running around in the oak tree before it became a table," Jamie says.

"Sure," says Dad. "Probably birds and insects, too."

"What about that picture frame, Dad?" asks Megan.

"That wood came all the way from a tropical rain forest. It's mahogany. But in many places, rain forests are being cut down too quickly to grow back."

"Isn't paper made from wood, too?"

"You bet—lots and lots of wood. Think of all the trees in our books and newspapers and magazines."

"We can recycle that wood, can't we, Dad? And use the trees over and over?"

"Yes, indeed. As long as we don't use too much all at once, we can keep on making things out of trees."

"Where else can we go on our nature hike, Dad?"

"How about China?"

"China?" Megan laughs. "That's all the way around the world."

"No, it's right here. Follow me." The three hikers troop down the hall.

"Your mom's nightgown is made of silk from China. And silk is made by caterpillars. They spin it into cocoons."

"What about this sponge?" Jamie calls from the bathroom. "Did some animal make it?"

"That sponge used to *be* an animal. It lived at the bottom of the ocean."

"We sure have a lot of things that come from nature."

"Can you think of anything that doesn't?"

"Plastic!" cries Jamie, pointing to the shower curtain.

"Or is there a plastic tree?"

Dad laughs. "No, plastic comes from oil. But oil, gas, and coal come from plants that lived millions of years ago. The plants were buried for a very long time, and slowly they turned into oil, gas, and coal."

"So maybe the plastic in my pen came from a tree that a dinosaur chomped on," says Jamie.

"Maybe it did," Dad agrees.

"Is nature in everything, then?" Jamie asks.

"Yes, everything. The glass in the window is made from sand. The dishes are made from clay. The metal in your knife and spoon comes from rocks. Wherever we go, nature is all around us."

"Wow," says Megan. "We've traveled back millions of years and all over the world on this nature hike."

"Yeah," says Jamie. "I wonder where we'll go on our next one."

SEEING THE AIR

FINALLY, IT'S WARM enough to go swimming!" cries Jamie.

His mom dips her toe in the water. "Brr! It feels too cold to me."

"Not to me," Jamie says. "I'm going in to watch the fish."

"Me, too," says Megan.

"You've still got a cold, Megan. Better not," says Mom.

"But I'll miss all the fun."

"We can have fun," Mom says. "We can watch the air."

"The air! But there's nothing there."

"Sure, there is. Feel the wind? That's moving air. If we could see it, what would it look like?"

"Um . . . it would look like the ocean, and the birds would be swimming in it like fish!"

"That's a good answer. Yes, the air holds the birds up. It also holds up airplanes. And it pushes sails and wind-mills and makes the trees bend."

"And it steals beach umbrellas!" cries Megan.

"Whew! I'm out of breath," says Megan when she gets back.

"Running made your body need more air. But even when you're just sitting or sleeping, your body needs to breathe. Without air we would die."

"And plants need air, too," says Megan. "We learned all about it in school. Air is made of gases. Plants take in carbon dioxide, and they give off oxygen. Animals do the opposite—take in oxygen and breathe out carbon dioxide. Isn't it cool that plants and animals help each other like that?"

"Very cool," Mom agrees.

"But what about fish? How can they breathe?"

"They take oxygen from the water," says Mom.
"Fish breathe in oxygen through their gills."

"So when we use up all the air, where does the
new air come from?"

(24)

"We don't use it up. We use the same air over and over—the gases just get rearranged. We share the air with plants and other animals. It goes out of them and into you. And out of you and into them."

(25)

"Mom, why is that dog sniffing the air?" asks Megan.

"Because the air is carrying smells to his nose."

"What *is* a smell, anyway?"

"Actually, what we smell are tiny pieces of something. The pieces are so tiny we can't see them. Dogs can even smell pieces left behind from a person or animal that was here yesterday. Some animals leave smells to mark their territory. And some of those smells smell pretty bad to us."

"This flower smells nice," says Megan.

"Yes. Bees can smell the flowers, too. And when they come to get nectar to make their honey, they pollinate the flowers."

"Neat! So what else is in the air, Mom?"

"The air is full of sounds. Listen. What can you hear?"

"I can hear some birds, and I can hear Jamie laughing. And a frog."

"You have good ears, Megan. What you hear are vibrations that travel through the air like waves across the water."

"And did you know there is water in the air?" Mom asks.

"I know—especially in the clouds. That's where snow and rain come from. Look at all the clouds, Mom. There are way more now than before."

"Yes, the warm air is bringing them. This air came all the way from the tropics."

(30)

"You mean we could be breathing air from the Amazon jungle or from Africa?"

"Could be. Air really moves around. And so do clouds. Clouds are water that rose up into the air. So maybe the water in these clouds came from an ocean on the other side of the world, and strong winds blew them here."

31

"Does the air go all the way to the moon?" asks Megan.

"No, it stays close to Earth. The farther we go from Earth, the less air there is. Way out, a layer of gas called ozone protects us from a harmful part of sunlight. Farther away still, there is no air at all."

"I guess that's why astronauts take air with them."

"Right. Without it, they couldn't breathe."

"Uh-oh, I think it's going to rain," Mom says. "Come on, you two. It's time to go."

"I had so much fun," says Jamie. "I saw a school of little fish and some ducks floating on the water."

"We saw some amazing things, too," Megan tells him. "We saw the air."

"No way!" says Jamie. "That's impossible."

"Not really," says Megan. "You just need imagination."

TIME TRAVELERS

"COME ON, JAMIE! Mom and Dad are planting
the garden," Megan calls. "Let's help."

"Gardens are boring," Jamie grumbles. "Everything
takes so long to grow."

"Not if we do some time traveling," says Mom.
"Then we can make lots of exciting discoveries."

"What kind of discoveries?" Jamie asks.

"Well, see that dip in the ground that runs through our yard and all our neighbors' yards? A hundred years ago, before there were houses here, that was a creek."

"So fish used to swim here, and animals came to drink. I can almost see them," Jamie says, half-closing his eyes.

"I can go back further than that," says Dad.
"Look at the big rock I just dug up."

"Where did it come from, Dad?"

"Millions of years ago, even before there were
people on Earth, lava flowed out of volcanoes. It cooled
and hardened into rocks. Then, during one of the ice
ages, glaciers dragged the rocks a long way, and one of
them landed here. When the ice melted, the rock stayed."

"So when the ice was here, were there polar bears
in our yard?" asks Megan.

"No, our yard was buried under ice deeper than the
tallest skyscraper."

"Wow!" Jamie says. "Our yard is more interesting
than I thought!"

"Here's another clue to the past," Mom says.

"All I see is dirt," says Megan.

"Look closer," says Mom. "Most of the dirt is dark with lots of twigs and leaves in it. And some is made of tiny grains of sand. Each of these things comes from a different time."

"The sand is all that's left of old rocks that got worn down," Dad explains. "The twigs and leaves are much newer. And when we add the vegetable scraps from tonight's dinner, they will become part of the soil, too. But it will take a long time for them to break down."

"My friend Jenny found an arrowhead down where the creek used to be," says Megan.

"The aboriginal people who lived here shaped arrowheads out of stones," Dad says. "They likely used them for hunting the animals that lived by the water."

(45)

"Can we travel into the future, too?" asks Megan.

"Of course," says Dad. "These seeds we are planting will grow into vegetables that we'll eat over the summer. And the apple tree has blossoms now. In the fall, we'll be picking the fruit."

"Look," Jamie says, "there's a robin building a nest. In a few weeks there'll be baby birds in our yard. And there's a squirrel's nest."

"Right," says Dad. "Our backyard could have lots of babies in it soon."

(46)

"But what about hundreds of years from now? Or thousands!" says Megan.

"To figure that out, we have to use our imaginations," says Mom. "Maybe the city will get bigger, and there'll be highways and skyscrapers everywhere—maybe one right here in our yard."

"Or maybe the plants and animals will take over our house and yard," suggests Dad.

"What if pollution takes over?" asks Megan.

"Yes," Dad says, "that could happen if we're not careful."

"Then let's be careful. Let's make gardens instead of garbage."

"I like that idea," agrees Dad.

"I know!" Megan says. "Let's leave something here for time travelers in the future to find."

"Yeah!" Jamie cries. "Could we put something about us in a tin box and bury it in the garden?"

"That's a great idea," Mom says. "But let's use this glass jar instead. It won't rust away, and it could even be useful for those future finders. Let's all put something in it."

"I have a dime in my pocket," offers Jamie.

"I'm putting in my marble and the ring from Jenny's party," says Megan.

"And I'll add a story out of today's newspaper," says Mom.

"Wait for me! I'll be back in a minute." Dad rushes into the house. In no time he's back.

"It's a picture of us all," he says. On the bottom he writes: "The Backyard Time Travelers."

"I was just thinking," Megan says. "We've traveled inside, outside, around the world, and through time on our nature trips. I guess there's nowhere else to go."

"Sure there is," says Dad. "Nature is everywhere, so there is no end to the trips you can take. But you've made a very good start."

ACTIVITIES

A RAINY DAY HIKE

1) Look back through the pages of this chapter. Can you find other things in the pictures and guess where they came from? Here's a hint: on page 1, the shutters and window frames are made of wood from trees. (For more examples, see "Answers" on page 58.)

2) Take a nature walk in your own home. Find out what different things are made of and where they came from.

SEEING THE AIR

1) Look at the pictures again. How many other things can you "see" in the air? How does each one use air? Here's an example: on page 21 there is a hot-air balloon rising in the air. Why doesn't it fall? Because it is filled with air. (For more examples, see page 58.)

2) Create an "Amazing Air" book. Look for things around you that need air to live or to do a job—for example, houseplants and fans. List them in your book. Add a drawing, a photograph, or some writing to go with each one.

TIME TRAVELERS

1) Look back through these pages. Can you find more clues for the time travelers? Here's one: on page 37 there is a caterpillar on Dad's hand. What do you think it will become? Look through the other pages to find out. (For more clues to the past and future, see page 58.)

2) Ask an adult to help you send a message to the future. Maybe ten, fifty, or hundreds of years from now, other time travelers will find it.

GLOSSARY

ABORIGINAL PEOPLE The earliest known people to have lived in a region.

ANTENNAE Long, thin feelers on an insect's head. They are sensitive to touch and taste.

BACTERIA Creatures so small you can only see them with a microscope. Some are helpful, and some cause diseases.

BROMELIADS A group of short-stemmed tropical plants—for example, pineapples. Many bromeliads live on other plants and get water from the air and rain.

FUNGI A group of organisms such as mushrooms and mold. They are something like plants, but they reproduce by means of spores rather than seeds. (Singular is fungus.)

GILLS Breathing organs on a fish or other water animal. Gills take oxygen from the water.

GLACIER A huge sheet of slowly moving ice.

ICE AGE One of several times long ago when glaciers covered large areas of Earth. During the last ice age, glaciers covered much of North America.

LAVA Hot melted rock that flows out of volcanoes.

POLLINATE To carry pollen to a plant and cause it to reproduce. Insects such as bees pollinate by carrying grains of pollen from one flower to another.

TROPICAL RAIN FOREST A forest of broad-leaved evergreen trees growing in a hot, rainy area.

VOLCANO A mountain or hill with an opening from which lava, hot gases, and cinders sometimes shoot out from deep within Earth.

ANSWERS

Pages 2–3 The teddy bear is stuffed with kapok made of fibers from tree seeds.

4–5 The refrigerator is made of metal (from rocks) and plastic (from oil).

6–7 How many animals can you name?

8–9 The tropical animals are a jaguar, spider monkey, toucan, and leaf-cutter ant. The plants around the mahogany tree include orchids and bromeliads. Can you find the hummingbird?

11 The picture frame is bamboo, whose leaves pandas like to eat.

12–13 The tub and sink are metal (from rocks) and porcelain (from clay).

14–15 The radiator gives heat, and the electric lamp gives light. Heat and electricity sometimes come from oil, gas, or coal. Some electricity is made by water flowing over large dams.

16 The cereal is oats, and the pancakes and bread are made with wheat. Cocoa is made from the seeds of the cacao plant, and maple syrup is sap from a maple tree.

20–21 Air flows over and under the birds' wings, holding them up. Jamie blows air into soap bubbles. He has filled his raft with air so that it will float.

24–25 Beavers, frogs, and turtles take a breath of air above water and hold it. The lily pads "breathe" through pores on the tops of their leaves. How does Jamie breathe underwater?

26–27 The smell of rotting fish attracts house-flies. The skunk protects itself by releasing a strong-smelling liquid from a gland near its tail. Bees smell with their antennae.

29 Megan can also hear a turtle splashing and a squirrel chattering.

30–31 Water is evaporating from lakes and oceans. When it cools, it forms droplets that fall to Earth as rain or snow.

32–33 In space, there is no air and meteor-oids travel very fast. When they reach Earth's atmosphere, the air causes them to burn up. They are called meteorites when they hit the ground.

34–35 Grass, leaves, seeds, water, clothing, and hair are being moved by the wind. Why is it helpful for seeds to be blown about?

40 Long ago, volcanoes are erupting and rocks are being formed.

42–43 Soil is formed when living things die and decay. Animals, fungi, and bacteria break down dead plants into smaller and smaller pieces. Earthworms eat the soil, passing many tons of it through their bodies each year.

48–49 The city has spread over Megan and Jamie's backyard. What has happened to the plants and animals?

50–51 Two different ways the future might look. Which would you choose? What can you do to help that choice come true?